But it was only Bedtime Bear singing the birds to sleep.

Surround Bedtime Bear with all of the bird stickers.

"Look!" said Bedtime Bear. "There's your rainbow."
"No, that's Love-a-lot Bear painting," said Cheer Bear.

Find the sticker of the rainbow paint bucket and give it to Love-a-lot Bear.

Love-a-lot Bear thought she saw Cheer Bear's rainbow.
But it was only Friend Bear carrying a bouquet of flowers.

Look for the sticker of Friend Bear carrying flowers and add it to this page.

"I've spotted your rainbow!" cried Friend Bear.
"No," said Cheer Bear. "Those are Good Luck Bear's
butterflies."

Surround
Good Luck Bear
with all of the
butterfly stickers.

"Over there is the rainbow," said Good Luck Bear.
But Good Luck Bear had mistaken Funshine Bear's
balloons for the rainbow.

Find the
balloon stickers
and add them to
Funshine Bear's
balloons.

"There it is!" said Funshine Bear. "There's your rainbow!"

"That's not a rainbow, either." Cheer Bear sighed.

"That's Share Bear bringing lollipops for everyone."

Add the sticker
of Share Bear
carrying lollipops
to this page.

Share Bear thought she saw Cheer Bear's rainbow
just above the clouds.
But it turned out to be Tenderheart Bear's roller skates.

*Put the
roller skate
stickers on
Tenderheart Bear.*

"Look up in the sky," said Tenderheart Bear. "There is your rainbow."

"No. Those are raindrops," Cheer Bear said sadly.

Can you put
all of the
heart-shaped
raindrop stickers
in the sky?

"I just knew it was going to rain today," said Grumpy Bear.
"That's why I brought my umbrella."

Grumpy Bear
needs his umbrella.
Can you give
it to him?